Sugar  Spice

This is Sugar.

Those pancakes were good.

Now I can read my book.

Her cat, Bell, sneaks out.

Bell! No!

Pal sees Bell.

Bell, come back!

Pal! No!

BARK! BARK!

MEOW!

Bell runs up a tree.

My cat!

Bell and Pal get into Sugar's clothes.

The Big Show

At school:

What will I do?

What will I do?

At Spice's house:

I will sing in the show.

Spice sings for Sugar.

That was good!

Back at Spice's house:

Will you try out again?

Why? It will be the same.

Not if we are a team this time!

Sugar and Spice work on their new act.

At the big show:

At the Mall

Spice is bored with her games.

Sugar is bored with her books.

Sugar calls Spice.

Do you want to come over and play?

Yes!

But they are still bored.

We need new stuff.

We can go to the mall.

At the mall, they see a nice coat.

And they look at a pretty dress.

Then they see a stand.

Sugar and Spice put the toys away.

This is fun!

The store owner wants to pay them.

We just wanted to help.

No, thank you.

After they leave the store:

TOYS

Wait! We can use that money to help the kids in need.

They go back to the store.

Then, they go back to the stand.

Now we can help!

Thank you very much.